1

SAM DOWLING
Is a Dublin-born playwright. He has written and produced nearly thirty plays or small-cast versions of classics for Praxis Theatre Laboratory. His subject-matter has ranged from Irish history through the lives of writers and artists to re-working of themes from the Greek myths. His play about the Brontës ( co-written with Andrea Bird ) has had three productions in Tokyo.
For more detail see listing in playwrights' database at www.doollee.com

PRAXIS THEATRE LABORATORY is an experimental theatre which seeks its direction from the actors' response to the work. No-one takes on a separate role as director. We particularly value images conjured in rehearsal, and intuitive and emotional rather than intellectual or technical evaluation. We try to fix as little as possible and each performance retains an element of improvisation.
Founded by Sam Dowling as the in-house company at The Tabard in West London from 1984, in 1990 we left to pursue more experimental goals. We opened a small theatre space in County Roscommon, Ireland in 1999 and have toured UK, USA, Ireland, Belgium, Netherlands, Ukraine and Poland.

This version of MACBETH first performed at The Old Courthouse
Theatre, Frenchpark, County Roscommon in November 2001, with this
cast of eight:

DUNCAN ...................................................................................Shane Gately

MALCOLM .....................................................................................Gillian Rea

MACBETH ...........................................................................Patrick Brennan

BANQUO.................................................................................Shane Larkin

LADY MACBETH.....................................................................Maria Straw

PORTER...............................................................Alex Cusack (doubling)

MACDUFF..........................................................Shane Gately (doubling)

WITCHES...........................................Carol Brophy
                                                  Elaine Murphy
                                                  Alex Cusack

The WITCHES and  CAST doubling as
ROSS, LENNOX, SEYTON and OTHER LORDS
SOLDIERS
SERVANTS
DOCTOR
MURTHERERS

**Designed by Claire Harvey**

For performance permission and terms, contact Sam Dowling.

IRISH PLAYS AND OTHERS BY SAM DOWLING
IN PRINT AT WWW.LULU.COM OR IN THE PIPELINE

RIVERMAN [ Walter Greaves, naïf painter, rise and fall.]
CAULDRON OF BRONTËS [ Genius siblings.]
A SEASON IN HELL [ Wild poets Rimbaud and Verlaine.]
MOUNTAIN [ Life-changing encounters]
RENEWAL [ Site-specific version of MOUNTAIN]
TROJAN WOMEN
BIRTH OF THE BEAST [ Northern Ireland.]
BIG FELLA! [Michael Collins.]
ALLEGIANCE [ IRA in London.]
ANTIGONE
THE FLAME AND THE STONE [ Yeats and Maud Gonne.]
VIRGIN OF NOTTING HILL [ Sexual problems.]
ORESTEIAN TRILOGY
LOVELOST [ Abuse ]
RED COUNTESS GREEN CROW [Markievicz and O'Casey]
HA! HA! HA! [ Improvisations on Coward and Shakespeare.]



AND SMALL-CAST VERSIONS OF THESE CLASSICS;

THE CENCI
IMPORTANCE OF BEING EARNEST
CHERRY ORCHARD
THREE SISTERS
HEDDA GABLER
WHEN WE DEAD AWAKEN
HAMLET
MACBETH
ANTONY AND CLEOPATRA
THE TEMPEST

IRISH PLAYS AND OTHERS  Vol. 13

SHAKESPEARE'S

# MACBETH

A VERSION FOR EIGHT ACTORS
by
Sam Dowling

2001

Sam Dowling
85 Haddo House
Haddo Street
London SE10 9SE

E-mail praxis.lab@ntlworld.com

Published by Lulu 2007

www.lulu.com

© Sam Dowling 2001

ISBN 978-1-84799-092-1

# MACBETH

## (With a company of eight actors)

# dramatis personae

**DUNCAN     King Of Scotland

MALCOLM his son

MACBETH  general in the King's army

BANQUO        "        "      "            "         "

MACDUFF        "        "      "        "        "

LADY  MACBETH

WITCHES

**ROSS, LENNOX, SEYTON  and OTHER LORDS

**SOLDIERS

**SERVANTS

**DOCTOR

**MURTHERERS

**PORTER

**[ Note re Doubling.
MACDUFF might double as DUNCAN
BANQUO and WITCHES might double as ROSS, LENNOX, SEYTON
and OTHER LORDS, DOCTOR, MURDERERS,  SERVANTS, SOLDIERS
and PORTER.]

# PART ONE

[Thunder and Lightning ]

1st WITCH
When shall we three meet again
In thunder lightning or in rain

2nd WITCH
When the hurly-burly's done
When the battle's lost and won

3rd WITCH
That will be ere the set of sun

1st WITCH
Where the place

2nd WITCH
Upon the Heath

3rd WITCH
There to meet with Macbeth

1st WITCH
I come Graymalkin

ALL
Paddock calls anon
Fair is foul and foul is fail
Hover through the fog and filthy  air

[ EXEUNT
ENTER DUNCAN and MALCOLM ]

MALCOLM
....Then your Majesty, brave Macbeth (well he deserves that name)
Disdaining Fortune with his brandished steel

Which smoked with bloody execution
(Like Valour's minion) carved out his passage
Till he faced the slave
Which ne'er shook hands nor bade farewell to him
Till he unseamed him from the nave to th' chops
And fixed his head upon our battlements
Then mark father King of Scotland mark
How the Norweyan Lord surveying vantage
With furbished arms and new supplies of men
Began a fresh assault

DUNCAN
Dismayed not this our Captains Macbeth and Banquo

MALCOLM
Yes as sparrows eagles or the hare the lion
If I say sooth I must report they were
As cannons overcharged with double cracks
So they doubly redoubled strokes upon the foe
Except they meant to bathe in reeking wounds
Or memorize another Golgotha
Norway himself with terrible numbers
Assisted by that most disloyal traitor
The Thane of Cawdor began a dismal conflict
Till that Bellona's bridegroom lapped in proof
Confronted him with self-comparisons
Point against point rebellious arms 'gainst arms
Curbing his lavish spirit and to conclude
The victory fell on us

DUNCAN
No more that Thane of Cawdor shall deceive
Our bosom interest go pronounce his present death
And with his former title greet Macbeth

MALCOLM
I'll see it done

DUNCAN
What he hath lost noble Macbeth hath won

[ EXEUNT
ENTER WITCHES ]

1ˢᵗ WITCH
Where hast thou been sister

2ⁿᵈ WITCH
Killing swine

3ʳᵈ WITCH
Sister thou

1ˢᵗ WITCH
A sailor's wife had chestnuts in her lap
And mounched and mounched and mounched
Give me quote I
Aroint thee witch the rump-faced ronyon cries
Her husband's to Aleppo gone Master o' the *Tiger*
But in a sieve I'll thither sail
And like a rat without a tail
I'll do I'll do and I'll do

2ⁿᵈ WITCH
I'll give thee a wind

1ˢᵗ WITCH
Th'art kind

3ʳᵈ WITCH
And I another

1ˢᵗ WITCH
I myself have all the other
And the very ports they blow
All the quarters that they know
In the shipman's card
I'll drain him dry as hay

13

Sleep shall neither night nor day
Hang upon his pent-house lid
He shall live a man forbid
Weary seven nights nine times nine
Shall he dwindle peak and pine
Though his bark cannot be lost
Yet it shall be tempest-tossed

2<sup>nd</sup> WITCH
Show me show me

1<sup>st</sup> WITCH
Here I have a pilot's thumb
Wracked as homeward he did come

[ DRUM within.]

3<sup>rd</sup> WITCH
A drum a drum
Macbeth doth come

ALL
The Weird Sisters hand in hand
Posters of the sea and land
Thus do go about about
Thrice to thine and thrice to mine
And thrice again to make up nine
Peace the charm's wound up

[ ENTER MACBETH and BANQUO ]

MACBETH
So foul and fair a day I have not seen

BANQUO
How far is it called to Forres. What are these
So withered and so wild in their attire
That look not like th' inhabitants o' th' earth
And yet are on 't. Live you or are you aught

14

That man may question.  You seem to understand me
By each at once upon her choppy fingers laying
Upon her skinny lips you should be women
And yet your beards forbid me to interpret
That you are so

MACBETH
Speak if you can what are you

1st WITCH
All hail Macbeth hail to thee Thane of Glamis

2nd WITCH
All hail Macbeth hail to thee Thane of Cawdor

3rd WITCH
All hail Macbeth that shall be King hereafter

BANQUO
Good sir why do you start and seem to fear
Things that do sound so fair.  I' th' name of truth
Are ye fantastical or that indeed
Which outwardly show.  My noble partner
You greet with present grace and great prediction
Of noble having and of royal hope
That he seems wrapt withal to me you speak not.
If you can look upon the seeds of Time
And say which seeds will grow and which will not
Speak then to me who neither beg nor fear
Your favours nor your hate

1st WITCH
Hail

2nd WITCH
Hail

3rd WITCH
Hail

**1st WITCH**

Lesser than Macbeth and greater

**2nd WITCH**

Not so happy yet much happier

**3rd WITCH**

Thou shall get Kings though thou be none
So all hail Macbeth and Banquo

**1st WITCH**

Banquo and Macbeth all hail

**MACBETH**

Stay you imperfect speakers tell me more
By Sinel's death I know I am Thane of Glamis
But how of Cawdor the Thane of Cawdor lives
A prosperous gentleman and to be King
Stands not within the prospect of belief
No more than to be Cawdor.  Say from whence
You owe this strange intelligence or why
Upon this blasted Heath you stop our way
With such prophetic greeting
Speak I charge you

[ WITCHES VANISH]

**BANQUO**

The earth hath bubbles as the water has
And these are of them whither are they vanished

**MACBETH**

Into the air and what seemed corporal
Melted as breath into the wind
Would they had stayed

**BANQUO**

Were such things here as we do speak about
Or have we eaten on the insane root
That takes the reason prisoner

MACBETH
Your children shall be Kings

BANQUO
You shall be King

MACBETH
And Thane of Cawdor too went it not so

BANQUO
To the selfsame words and tune who's here

[ENTER LORD.]

LORD
The King hath happily received Macbeth
The news of thy success and I am sent
To give thee from our Royal Master thanks
Only to herald thee into his sight
Not pay thee
And for an earnest of a great honour
He bade from him call thee Thane of Cawdor
In which addition hail thee worthy Thane
For it is thine

BANQUO
What can the Devil speak true

MACBETH
The Thane of Cawdor lives
Why do you dress me in borrowed robes

LORD
Who was the Thane lives yet
But under heavy judgement bears that life
Which he deserves to lose
For treasons capital have overthrown him

BANQUO
Glamis and Thane of Cawdor
The greatest is behind but tis strange
And oftentimes to win us to our harm
The instruments of darkness tell us truths
Win us with honest trifles to betray's
In deeper consequence

MACBETH
I thank you sir
This supernatural soliciting
Cannot be ill cannot be good
If ill why hath it given me earnest of success
Commencing in a truth I am Thane of Cawdor
If good why do I yield to that suggestion
Whose horrid image doth unfix my hair
And make my seated heart knock at my ribs
Against the use of nature. Present fears
Are less than horrible imaginings
My thought whose murther yet is but fantastical
Shakes so my single state of man
That function is smothered in surmise
And nothing is but what is not

BANQUO
Look how my partner's wrapt

MACBETH
If Chance will have me king
Why Chance may crown me
Without my stir

BANQUO
New honours come upon him
Like our strange garments cleave not to their mould
But with the aid of use

MACBETH
Come what come may

Time and the hour runs through the roughest day
Let us towards the King
Come

[ EXEUNT.


KING DUNCAN, attended, MALCOLM ]


DUNCAN
Is execution done on Cawdor


MALCOLM
My liege I have spoken with one who saw him die
Who did report that frankly he
Confessed his treasons implored your Highness' pardon
And set forth a deep repentance
Nothing in his life became him
Like the leaving of it.  He died
As one that had been studied in his death
To throw away the dearest thing he owned
As 'twere a careless trifle


DUNCAN
There's no art
To find the mind's construction in the face
He was a gentleman on whom I built
An absolute trust

[ ENTER
MACBETH, BANQUO etc.]
O worthiest cousin
The sin of my ingratitude even now
Was heavy on me.  Thou art so far before
That swift wing of recompense is slow
To overtake thee.  Would thou had less deserved
That the proportion both of thanks and payment
Might have been mine only I have left to say
More is thy due than more than all can pay


MACBETH
The service and the loyalty I owe

In doing it pays itself
Your Highness' part is to receive our duties
And our duties are to your throne and state
Children and servants which do but what they should
By doing every thing safe towards your love
And honour

DUNCAN
Welcome hither
I have begun to plant thee and will labour
To make thee full of growing. Noble Banquo
That hast no less deserved nor must be known
No less to have done so let me enfold thee
And hold thee to my heart

BANQUO
There if I grow
The harvest is your own

DUNCAN
My plenteous joys
Wanton in fulness seek to hide themselves
In drops of sorrow.  Sons kinsmen Thanes
And you whose places are the nearest know
We will establish our estate upon
Our eldest Malcolm whom we name hereafter
The Prince of Cumberland which honour must
Not unaccompanied invest him only
But signs of nobleness like stars shall shine
On all deservers.  From hence to Inverness
And bind us further to you

MACBETH
The rest is labour which is not used for you
I'll be myself the harbinger and make joyful
The hearing of my wife with your approach
So humbly take my leave

DUNCAN
My worthy Cawdor

MACBETH
The Prince of Cumberland that is a step
On which I must fall down or else o'erleap
For in my way it lies.  Stars hide your fires
Let not light see my black and deep desires
The eye wink at the hand yet let that be
Which the eye fears when it is done to see
[ FLOURISH.  EXEUNT.


LADY MACBETH with a letter.]


LADY MACB
This is great news Macbeth
Glamis thou art and Cawdor and shall be
What thou art promised yet do I fear thy nature
It is too full o' the milk o' humane kindness
To catch the nearest way. Thou wouldst be great
Art not without ambition but without
The illness should attend it.  What thou wouldst highly
That wouldst thou holily wouldst not play false
And yet wouldst wrongly win
Thou 'ldst have great Glamis that which cries
Thus thou must do if thou have it
And that which rather thou dost fear to do
Thou wishest should be undone. Hie thee hither
That I may pour my spirits in thy ear
And chastise with the valour of my tongue
All that impedes thee from the golden round
Which Fate and metaphysical aid doth seem
To have thee crowned withal

.....

....

The raven himself is hoarse
That croaks the fatal entrance of Duncan
Under my battlements. Come you spirits
That tend on human thoughts unsex me here

21

And fill me from the crown to the toe top-full
Of direst cruelty make thick my blood
Stop up the access and passage to remorse
That no compunctious  visitings of Nature
Shake my fell purpose nor keep peace between
Th' effect and it. Come to my  woman's breasts
And take my milk for gall you murth'ring ministers
Wherever in your sightless substances
You wait on Nature's mischief. Come thick Night
And pall thee in the dunnest smoke of Hell
That my keen knife see not the wound it makes
Nor Heaven peep through the blanket of the dark
To cry hold hold

[ Enter MACBETH]

Great Glamis worthy Cawdor
Greater than both by the all-hail hereafter
Thy letters have transported me beyond
This ignorant present and I feel now
The future in the instant

MACBETH
My dearest love
Duncan comes here tonight

LADY MACB
And when goes hence

MACBETH
Tomorrow as he purposes

LADY MACB
O never
Shall sun that morrow see
Your face my Thane is like a book where men
May read strange matters to beguile the time
Look like the time bear welcome in your eye
Your hand your tongue look like th' innocent flower
But be the serpent under 't. He that's coming
Must be provided for and you shall put

This nights's great business into my dispatch
Which shall to all our nights and days to come
Give solely sovereign sway and masterdom

MACBETH
We will speak further

LADY MACB
Only look up clear
To alter favour ever is to fear
Leave all the rest to me

[EXEUNT

MUSIC and LIGHTS.
KING DUNCAN attended,
MALCOLM, BANQUO.]

DUNCAN
This castle hath a pleasant seat
The air nimbly and sweetly recommends itself
Unto our gentle senses

BANQUO
This guest of summer
The temple-haunting martlet does approve
By this loved mansionry that the Heaven's breath
Smells wooingly here no jutty frieze
Buttress nor coign of vantage but this bird
Hath made his pendant bed and procreant cradle
Where they most breed and haunt I have observed
The air is delicate
[ ENTER LADY MACBETH ]

DUNCAN
See see our honoured hostess
The love that follows us sometimes is our trouble
Which still we thank as love. Herein I teach you
How you shall bid God 'ild us for your pains
And thank us for your trouble

LADY MACB
All our service
In every point twice done and then done double
Were poor and single business to contend
Against those honours deep and broad
Wherewith your Majesty loads our House
For those of old and the late dignities
Heaped up to them we rest your hermits

DUNCAN
Where's the Thane of Cawdor
We coursed him at the heels and had a purpose
To be his purveyor but he rides well
And his great love ( sharp as his spur ) hath holp him
To his home before us fair and noble hostess
We are your guest tonight

LADY MACB
Your servants ever
Have theirs themselves and what is theirs in compt
To make their audit at your Highness' pleasure
Still to return your own

DUNCAN
Give me your hand
Conduct me to mine host we love him highly
And shall continue our graces towards him
By your leave hostess

[ EXEUNT.

MUSIC and A FEAST being served
ENTER MACBETH.]

MACBETH
If it were done when 'tis done then 'twere well
It were done quickly if the assassination
Could trammel up the consequence and catch
With his surcease success that but this blow
Might be the be-all and the end-all. Here

But here upon this bank and school of time
We'd jump the life to come.  But in these cases
We still have judgement here that we but teach
Bloody instructions which being taught return
To plague the inventor.  This even-handed Justice
Commends the ingredients of our poisoned chalice
To our own lips.  He's here in double trust
First as I am his kinsman and his subject
Strong both against the deed then as his host
Who should against his murtherer shut the door
Not bear the knife myself. Besides this Duncan
Hath borne his faculties so meek hath been
So clear in his great office that his virtues
Will plead like angels trumpet-tongued against
The deep damnation of his taking off
And Pity like a naked new-born babe
Striding the blast or Heaven's cherubin horsed
Upon the sightless couriers of the air
Shall blow the horrid deed in every eye
That tears shall drown the wind. I have no spur
To prick the sides of my intent but only
Vaulting Ambition which o'erleaps itself
And fall on t'other

[ENTER LADY MACBETH ]

How now  what news


LADY MACB
He has almost supped why have you
Left the chamber


MACBETH
Hath he asked for me


LADY MACB
Know you not he has


MACBETH
We will proceed no further in this business
He hath honoured me of late and I have bought

Golden opinions from all sorts of people
Which would be worn now in their newest gloss
Not cast aside so soon

LADY MACB
Was the hope drunk
Wherein you dressed yourself. Hath it slept since
And wakes it now to look so green and pale
At what it did so freely.  From this time
Such I account thy love.  Art thou afeared
To be the same in thine own act and valour
As thou art in desire. Wouldst thou have that
Which thou esteemest the ornament of life
And live a coward in thine own esteem
Letting I dare not wait upon I would
Like the poor cat in the adage

MACBETH
Prithee peace
I dare do all that does become a man
Who dares do more is none

LADY MACB
What beast was it then
That made you break this enterprise to me
When you durst do it when you were a man
And to be more than what you were you would
Be so much more than the man. Nor time nor place
Did then adhere and yet you would make both
They have made themselves and that their fitness now
Does unmake you.  I have given suck and know
How tender 'tis to love the babe that milks me
I would while it was smiling in my face
Have plucked my nipple from his boneless gums
And dashed the brains out had I so sworn
As you have done to this

MACBETH
If we should fail

LADY MACB

We fail ?

But screw your courage to the sticking-place
And we'll not fail when Duncan is asleep
(Whereto the rather shall his day's hard journey
Soundly invite him ) his two chamberlains
Will I with wine and wassail so convince
That memory the warder of the brain
Shall be a fume and the receipt of reason
A limbeck only when in swinish sleep
Their drenched natures lie as in a death
What cannot you and I perform upon
Th' unguarded Duncan. What not put upon
His spongy officers who shall bear the guilt
Of our great quell

MACBETH

Bring forth men-children only
For thy undaunted mettle shall compose
Nothing but males.  Will it not be received
When we have marked with blood those sleepy two
Of his own chamber and used their very daggers
That they have done it

LADY MACB

Who dares receive it other
As we shall make our griefs and clamour roar
Upon his death

MACBETH

I am settled and bend up
Each corporal agent to this terrible feat
Away and mock the time with fairest show
False face must hide what the false heart doth know

[ EXEUNT.]

# PART TWO

[ BANQUO.]

## BANQUO
The moon is down
There's husbandry in Heaven
Their candles are all out
A heavy summons lies like lead upon me
And yet I would not sleep
Powers restrain in me the cursed thoughts
That Nature gives way to in repose

[ENTER MACBETH.]

Who's there

## MACBETH
A friend

## BANQUO
What sir not yet at rest. The King's abed
He hath been in unusual pleasure
And sent forth great largess to your offices
This diamond he greets your wife withal
By the name of most kind hostess
And shut up in measureless content

## MACBETH
Being unprepared
Our will became the servant to defect
Which else should free have wrought

## BANQUO
All's well
I dreamt last night of the three weird sisters
To you they have shown some truth

## MACBETH
I think not of them
Yet when we can entreat an hour to serve

28

We would spend it in some words upon that business
If you would grant the time

BANQUO
At your kindest leisure

MACBETH
If you shall cleave to my consent
When 'tis it shall make honour for you

BANQUO
So I lose none
In seeking to augment it but keep still
My bosom franchised and allegiance clear
I shall be counselled

MACBETH
Good repose the while

BANQUO
Thanks sir the like to you     [ EXIT]

MACBETH
Is this a dagger which I see before me
The handle towards my hand. Come let me clutch thee
I have thee not and yet I see thee still
Art thou not fatal vision sensible
To feeling as to sight or art thou but
A dagger of the mind a false creation
Proceeding from the heat-oppressed brain
I see thee yet in form as palpable
As this which now I draw
Thou marshalled me the way that I was going
And such an instrument I was to use
Mine eyes are made the fools of the other senses
Or else worth all the rest I see thee still
And on thy blade and dudgeon gouts of blood
Which was not so before.  There's no such thing

It is the bloody business which informs
Thus to mine eyes. Now o'er the one half-world
Nature seems dead and wicked dreams abuse
The curtained sleep witchcraft celebrates
Pale Hecate's offerings and withered Murther
Alarumed by his wicked sentinel the wolf
Whose howl's his watch thus with his stealthy pace
With Tarquin's ravishing strides towards his design
Moves like a ghost. Thou sure and firm-set Earth
Hear not my steps which way they walk for fear
Thy very stones prate of my whereabout
And take the present horror from the time
Which now suits with it. Whilst I threat he lives
Words to the heat of deeds  too cold breath gives

[ A BELL RINGS.]

I go and it is done the bell invites me
Hear it not Duncan for it is a knell
That summons thee to Heaven or to Hell

[EXIT. ENTER LADY MACBETH.]


LADY MACB

That which had made them drunk hath made me bold
What hath quenched them hath given me fire
Hark peace it was the owl that shrieked
The fatal bellman which gives the sternest goodnight
He is about it the doors are open
And the surfeited grooms do mock their charge
With snores. I have drugged their possets
And Death and Nature do contend about them
Whether they live or die

[ ENTER MACBETH }


MACBETH
Who's there  hoa


LADY MACB
Alack I am afraid they have awaked
And 'tis not done the attempt and not the deed
Confounds us hark I laid their daggers ready

30

He could not miss 'em. Had he not resembled
My father as he slept I had done it
My husband

MACBETH
I have dome the deed
Didst thou not hear a noise

LADY MACB
I heard the owl scream and the crickets cry
Did not you speak

MACBETH
When

LADY MACB
Now

MACBETH
As I descended

LADY MACB
Ay

MACBETH
Hark who lies in the second chamber

LADY MACB
Malcolm and Banquo

MACBETH
This is a sorry sight

LADY MACB
A foolish thought to say a sorry sight

MACBETH
There's one did laugh in his sleep
And one cried Murther that they did wake each other

I stood and heard them but they did say their prayers
And addressed them again to sleep

LADY MACB
There are the two lodged together

MACBETH
One cried God bless us and Amen the other
As they had seen me with these hangman's hands
Listening their fear I could not say Amen
When they did say God bless us

LADY MACB
Consider it not so deeply

MACBETH
But wherefore could not I pronounce Amen
I had most need of blessing and Amen stuck in my throat

LADY MACB
These deeds must not be thought
After these ways so it will make us mad

MACBETH
Methought I heard a voice cry Sleep no more
Macbeth doth murther Sleep the innocent sleep
Sleep that knits up the ravelled sleave of care
The death of each day's life sore labour's bath
Balm of hurt minds great Nature's second course
Chief nourisher in Life's feast

LADY MACB
What do you mean

MACBETH
Still it cried Sleep no more to all the House
Glamis hath murthered Sleep and therefore Cawdor
Shall sleep no more Macbeth shall sleep no more

LADY MACB

Who was it that thus cried. Why worthy Thane
You do unbend your noble strength to think
So brain-sickly of such things go get some water
And wash this filthy witness from your hand
Why did you bring these daggers from the place
They must lie there go carry them and smear
The sleepy grooms with blood

MACBETH

I'll go no more
I am afraid to think what I have done
Look on it again I dare not

LADY MACB

Infirm of purpose
Give me the daggers the sleeping and the dead
Are but as pictures 'tis the eye of childhood
That fears a painted devil. If he do bleed
I'll guild the faces of the grooms withal
For it must seem their guilt

[EXIT.
KNOCKING WITHIN.]

MACBETH

Whence is that knocking
How is't with me when every noise appalls me
What hands are here hah they pluck out mine eyes
With all great Neptune's Ocean wash this blood
Clean from my hand. No this hand will rather
The multitudinous seas incarnadine
Making the green one red
[ ENTER LADY MACBETH]

LADY MACB

My hands are of your colour but I shame
To wear a heard so white   [ KNOCK.]
I hear a knocking at the south entry
Retire we to our chamber

A little water clears us of this deed
How easy is it then. Your constancy
Hath left you unattended

[ KNOCK ]

Hark more knocking
Get on your nightgown let occasion call us
And show us to be watchers be not lost
So poorly in your thoughts


MACBETH
To know my deed

[ KNOCK ]

Twere best not know myself
Wake Duncan with thy knocking
I would thou couldst.

[ EXEUNT.
ENTER PORTER
KNOCKING WITHIN.]

PORTER
Here's a knocking indeed
If a man were Porter of Hell Gate
He should have old turning the key [KNOCK]
Knock knock knock Who's there in the name of Beelzebub
Here's a farmer that hanged himself on the expectation of plenty
Come in time have napkins enow about you here you'll sweat for it
[KNOCK}

Knock knock Who's there in the other Devil's name
Faith here's another equivocator
That could swear in both scales against either scale
Who committed treason enough for God's sake
Yet could not equivocate to Heaven
Oh come in equivocator [KNOCK]
Knock knock knock [KNOCK]
Anon anon I pray you remember the porter
[ENTER MACDUFF]


MACDUFF
Was it so late friend ere you went to bed that you do lie so late


34

PORTER
Faith sir we were carousing till the second cock and drink sir
Is a great provoker of three things

MACDUFF
What three things does drink especially promote

PORTER
Marry sir nose-painting sleep and urine
Lechery sir it provokes and unprovokes
It provokes the desire and takes away the performance
Therefore much drink may be said to be an equivocator with lechery
It makes him and it mars him it sets him on and it takes him off
It persuades him and disheartens him makes him stand to and not
stand to
In conclusion equivocates him in a sleep and giving him the lie leaves
him

MACDUFF
I believe drink gave thee the lie last night

PORTER
That it did sir i' the very throat on me
But I requited him for his lie and (I think ) being too strong for him
Though he took up my legs sometime
Yet I made a shift to cast him [ENTER MACBETH.]

MACDUFF
Is thy master stirring
Our knocking has awaked him here he comes
Good morrow noble sir

MACBETH
Good morrow

MACDUFF
Is the King stirring worthy Thane

MACBETH
Not yet

MACDUFF
He did command me to call timely on him
I have almost slipped the hour

MACBETH
I'll bring you to him

MACDUFF
I know this is a joyful trouble to you but yet 'tis one

MACBETH
The labour we delight in physics pain
This is the door

MACDUFF
I'll make so bold to call for 'tis my limited service [EXIT}

MACBETH
Twas a rough night

[ ENTER MACDUFF]

MACDUFF
O horror horror horror
Tongue nor heart cannot conceive nor name thee

MACBETH
What's the matter

MACDUFF
Confusion now hath made his masterpiece
Most sacrilegious murther hath broke ope
The Lord's anointed Temple and stole hence
The life o' the building

MACBETH
What is it you say the life

MACDUFF
Approach the chamber and destroy your sight
With a new Gorgon. Do not bid me speak
See and then speak yourselves awake awake [EXIT MACBETH}
Ring the alarum bell murther and treason
Lords Banquo Malcolm awake
Shake off this downy sleep Death's counterfeit
And look on Death itself up up and see
The great Doom's image Malcolm Banquo
As from your graves rise up and walk like sprites
To countenance this horror. Ring the bell
[BELL RINGS
ENTER LADY MACBETH.]
LADY MACB
What's the business
That such hideous trumpet calls to parley
The sleepers of this house speak speak

MACDUFF
O gentle Lady
'Tis not for you to hear what I can speak
The repetition to a woman's ear
Would murther as it fell [ENTER BANQUO }
O Banquo Banquo our Royal Master's murthered

LADY MACB
Woe alas
What in our house

BANQUO
Too cruel any where
Dear Duff I prithee contradict yourself
And say it is not so [ENTER MACBETH}

MACBETH
Had I but died an hour before this chance
I had lived a blessed time for from this instant
There's nothing serious in mortality
All is but toys Renown and Grace is dead

The wine of Life is drawn and the mere lees
Is left this vault to brag of [ENTER MALCOLM]

MALCOM
What's amiss

MACBETH
You are and do not know it
The spring the head the fountain of your blood
Is stopped the very source of it is stopped

MACDUFF
Your Royal Father's murthered

MALCOLM
O by whom

MACDUFF
Those of his chamber as it seemed had done it
Their hands and faces were all badged with blood
So were their daggers which unwiped we found
Upon their pillows they stared and were distracted
No man's life was to be trusted with them

MACBETH
O yet I do repent me of my fury that I did kill them

MACDUFF
Wherefor did you so

MACBETH
Who can be wise amazed temperate and furious
Loyal and neutral in a moment. No man
The expedition of my violent love
Outrun the pauser Reason. Here lay Duncan
His silver skin laced with his golden blood
And his gashed stabs looked like a breach in Nature
For Ruin's wasteful entrance there the murthers
Steeped in the colours of their trade their daggers

38

Unmannerly breeched with gore who could refrain
That had a heart to love and in that heart
Courage to make his love known

LADY MACB
Help me hence hoa

MACDUFF
Look to the Lady

MALCOLM
Why do I hold my tongue
That most may claim this argument for mine
Let me away my tears are not yet brewed
Nor my strong sorrow upon the foot of motion

BANQUO
Look to the Lady
And when we have our naked frailties laid
That suffer in exposure let us meet
And question this most bloody piece of work
To know it further. Fears and scruples shake us
In the great hand of God I stand and hence
Against the indivulged pretence I fight
Of treasonous malice

MACDUFF
And so do I

ALL
So all

MACBETH
Let's briefly put on manly readiness
And meet in the Hall together

ALL
Well contented     [ EXEUNT]

MALCOLM
What will I do
I'll not consort with them
To show an unfelt sorrow is an office
Which the false man does easy
I'll to England
This murtherous shaft that's shot
Hath not yet lighted and my safest way
Is to avoid the aim. Therefore to horse
And let me not be dainty of leave-taking
But shift away there's warrant in that theft
Which steals itself when there's no mercy left   [EXIT
ENTER MACDUFF ]
MACDUFF
Seest the Heavens as troubled with man's act
Threatens his bloody stage by the clock tis day
And yet dark Night strangles the travelling lamp
It's Night's predominance or the Day's shame
That Darkness does the face of Earth entomb
When living light should kiss it
Tis unnatural
Even like the deed that's done on Tuesday last
A falcon towering in her pride of place
Was by a mousing owl hawked at and killed
And Duncan's horses ( a thing most strange and certain)
Beauteous and swift the minions of their race
Turned wild in nature broke their stalls flung out
Contending 'gainst obedience as they would
Make war on mankind
'Tis said they eat each other
And Malcolm the King's heir and eldest son
Is stolen away and fled which puts upon him
Suspicion of the deed. 'Gainst Nature still
Thriftless Ambition that wilt ravin up
Thine own life's means then 'tis most like
The sovereignty will fall upon Macbeth
He is already named and gone to Scone
To be invested
Duncan's body carried to Colmkill

40

The sacred storehouse of his predecessors
And guardian of their bones
I'll to Fife
Well may we see things well done there adieu
Lest our old robes sit easier than our new
God's benison go with us and with those
Who would make good of bad and friends of foes   [EXIT]

# PART THREE

BANQUO
Thou has it now King Cawdor Glamis all
As the Weird Sisters promised and I fear
Thou play'dst most foully for it yet it was said
It should not stand in thy posterity
But that myself should be the root and father
Of many Kings. If there come truth from them
As upon thee Macbeth their speeches shine
Why by the verities on thee made good
May they not be my oracles as well
And set me up in hope.  But hush no more

[ SENNET SOUNDED.
ENTER MACBETH AS KING
and  LADY MACBETH, attended.]


MACBETH
Here's our chief guest


LADY MACB
If he had been forgotten
It had been as a gap in our great feast
And all-thing unbecoming


MACBETH
Tonight we'll hold a solemn supper sir
And I'll request your presence


BANQUO
Let your Highness
Command upon me to the which my duties
Are with a most dissoluble tie
For ever knit


MACBETH
Ride you this afternoon

BANQUO

Ay as far my Lord as will fill up the time
Twixt this and supper. Go not my horse the better
I must become a borrower of the night
For a dark hour or twain

MACBETH

Fail not our feast

BANQUO

My Lord I will not

MACBETH

We hear our bloody cousin is bestowed
In England and still not confessing
His cruel parricide filling his hearers
With strange invention. But of that tomorrow
When therewithal we shall have cause of state
Craving us jointly. Hie you to horse
Adieu till you return at night
Goes your son with you

BANQUO

Ay my good Lord our time does call upon us

MACBETH

Farewell

[ EXIT BANQUO.]

....

Bring those men before us

....

To be thus is nothing but to be safely thus
Our fears in Banquo stick deep
And in his royalty of nature reigns that
Which would be feared. Tis much he dares
And to that dauntless temper of his mind
He hath a wisdom that doth guide his valour
To act in safety. There is none but he
Whose being I do fear and under him

My Genius is rebuked as it is said
Mark Antony's was with Caesar. He chid the Sisters
When first they put the name of King upon me
And bad them speak to him. Then prophet-like
they hailed him father to a line of Kings
Upon my head they placed a fruitless crown
And put a barren sceptre in my gripe
Thence to be wrenched with an unlineal hand
No son of mine succeeding if it be so
For Banquo's issue have I fil'd my mind
For them the gracious Duncan have I murthered
Put rancours in the vessel of my peace
Only for them and mine eternal jewel
Given to the common Enemy of man
To make them kings the seeds of Banquo Kings
Rather than so come Fate into the list
And champion me to the utterance
Who's there

[ ENTER TWO MURTHERERS
HE speaks to servant OFF  ]

Now go to the door an and stay there till we call
....
Was it not yesterday we spoke together

1st MURTHERER
It was so please your Highness

MACBETH
Well then
Now we have considered of my speeches
Know that it was he in the times past
Which held you so under fortune
Which you thought had been our innocent self
This I made good to you in our last conference
Passed in probation with you
How you were borne in hand how crossed
The instruments who wrought with them

44

And all things else that might
To half a soul and to a notion crazed
Say  thus did Banquo

1st MURTHERER
You made it known to us

MACBETH
I did so

1st MURTHERER
We are men my Liege

MACBETH
Ay in the catalogue ye go for men
As hounds and greyhounds mongrels spaniels curs
Shoughs water-rugs and demi-wolves are clept
All by the name of dogs.
Now if you have a station in the file
Not in the worst rank of manhood say it
And I will put that business in your bosoms
Whose execution takes your enemy off
Grapples you to the heart and love of us
Who wear our health but sickly in his life
Which in his death were perfect

2nd MURTHERER
I am one my Leige
Whom the vile blows and buffets of the world
Hath so incensed that I am reckless what I do
To spite the world

1st MURTHERER
And I another
So weary with disasters tugged with Fortune
That I would set my life on any chance
To mend it or be rid on it

MACBETH
Both of you know Banquo was your enemy

BOTH
True my Lord

MACBETH
So is he mine and in such bloody distance
That every minute of his being thrusts
Against my nearest of life and though I could
With barefaced power sweep him from my sight
And bid my will avouch it yet I must not
For certain friends that are both his and mine
Whose loves I may not drop but wail his fall
Who I struck down and thence it is
That I to your assistance do make love
Masking the business from the common eye
For sundry weighty reasons

2nd MURTHERER
We shall my Lord
Perform what you command us

1st MURTHERER
Though our lives...

MACBETH
Your spirits shine through you
Within this hour at most
I will advise you where to plant yourselves
Acquaint you with the perfect spy of the time
The moment on it for it must be done tonight
And something from the palace always thought
That I require clearness and with him
To leave no rubs or botches in the work
Now his son that keeps him company
Whose absence is no less material to me
Than is his father's must embrace the fate
Of that dark hour resolve yourselves apart

I'll come to you anon

BOTH
We are resolved my Lord

MACBETH
I'll call upon you straight abide within
It is concluded Banquo thy soul's flight
If it find Heaven must find it out tonight

[ EXEUNT.
ENTER LADY MACBETH.]

LADY MACB
Nought's had all's spent
Where our desire is got without content
Tis safer to be that which we destroy
Than by destruction dwell in doubtful joy [ ENTER MACBETH]
How now my Lord why do you keep alone
Of sorriest fancies your companions making
Using those thoughts which should indeed have died
With them they think on things without all remedy
Should be without regard what's done is done

MACBETH
We have scorched the snake not killed it
She'll close and be herself whilst our poor malice
Remains in danger of her former tooth
But let the frame of things disjoint
Both the worlds suffer
Ere we will eat our meat in fear and sleep
In the affection of these terrible dreams
That shake us nightly better be with the dead
Whom we to gain our peace have sent to peace
Than on the torture of the mind to lie
In restless ecstasy
Duncan is in his grave
After life's fitful fever he sleeps well
Treason has done his worst nor steel nor poison
Malice domestic foreign levy nothing

Can touch him further

LADY MACB
Come on
Gentle my Lord sleek o'er your rugged looks
Be bright and jovial among your guests tonight

MACBETH
So shall I Love and so I pray be you
Let your remembrance apply to Banquo
Present him eminence both with eye and tongue
Unsafe the while that we must lave
Our honours in these flattering streams
And make our faces vizards to our hearts
Disguising what they are

LADFYMACB
You must leave this

MACBETH
O full of scorpions is my mind dear wife
Thou knowest that Baquo and his offspring lives

LADYMACB
But in them Nature's copy's not eterne

MACBETH
There's comfort yet they are assailable
Then be thou jocund ere the bat had flown
His cloistered flight ere to black Hecate's summons
The shard-borne beetle with his drowsy hums
Hath rung night's yawning peal
There shall be done a deed of dreadful note

LADY MACB
What's to be done

MACBETH
Be innocent of the knowledge dearest chuck

Till thou applaud the deed come seeling Night
Scarf up the tender eye of pitiful Day
And with thy bloody and invisible hand
Cancel and tear to pieces that great bond
Which keeps me pale.  Light thickens
And the crow makes wing to the rooky wood
Good things of Day begin to droop and drowse
Whiles Night's black agents to their preys do rouse
Thou marvellest at my words but hold thee still
Things bad begun make strong themselves by ill
So prithee go with me

[ EXEUNT
ENTER [Two or Three ?] MURTHERERS.
If three, use the original text]

1st MURTHERER
The West yet glimmers with some streaks of day
Now spurs the lated traveller apace
To gain the timely inn and near approaches
The subject of our watch

2nd MURTHERER
Hark I hear horses

BANQUO [WITHIN]
Give us a light there hoa

2nd MURTHERER
Then tis he
The rest that are within the nose of expectation
Already are in the Court

1st MURTHERER
His horses go about
Almost a mile but he does usually
So all men do from hence to the Palace Gate
Make it their walk

[ ENTER BANQUO followed [ OFF] by his SON
with a torch. ]

2nd MURTHERER
A light a light

1st MURTHERER
Tis he
Stand to it

BABQUO
It will be rain tonight

1st MURTHERER
Let it come down

BANQUO
O treachery
Fly my son fly fly fly
Thou mayest revenge. O slave

2nd MURTHERER
Who did strike out the light

1st MURTHERER
Was it not the way

2nd MURTHERER
There's but one down the son is fled

1st MURTHERER
We have lost
Best half of our affair

2nd MURTHERER
Well let's away and say how much is done

[ EXEUNT.

MACBETH and LADY MACBETH ,
a feast with numerous guests
MOSTLY  OFF.]

MACBETH

You know your own degrees sit down
At first and last the hearty welcome


LORDS

Thanks to your Majesty


MACBETH

Ourselves will mingle with society
And play the humble host
Our hostess keeps her state but in best time
We will require her welcome


LADY MACB

Pronounce it for me sir to all our friends
For my heart speaks they are welcome [ENTER 1st MURTHERER ]


MACBETH

See they encounter you with their hearts' thanks
Both sides are even here I'll sit in the midst
Be large in mirth anon we'll drink a measure
The table round.  There's blood upon thy face


1st MURTHERER

Tis Banquo's then


MACBETH

Tis better he without than he within
Is he dispatched


1st MURTHERER

My Lord his throat is cut that did I for him


MACBETH

Thou art the best of the cut-throats

Yet he's good that did the like for the son
If thou didst it thou art nonpareil

1st MURTHERER
Most Royal Sir
The son is 'scaped

MACBETH
Then come my fit again
I had else been perfect
Whole as the marble founded as the rock
As broad and general as the casing air
But now I am cabined cribbed confined bound in
To saucy doubts and fears. But Banquo's safe

1st MURTHERER
Ay my good Lord safe in a ditch he lies
With twenty trenched gashes on his head
The least a death to Nature

MACBETH
Thanks for that
There the grown serpent lies the worm that's fled
Hath nature that in time will venom breed
No teeth for the present. Get thee gone tomorrow
We'll hear ourselves again [ EXIT MURTHERER.]

LADY MACB
My Royal Lord
You do not give the cheer the feast is sold
That is not often vouched while tis a-making
Tis given with welcome to feed were best at home
From thence the sauce to meat is ceremony
Meeting were bare without it [ ENTER GHOST OF BANQUO
                                      sits in MACBETH's place.]

MACBETH
Sweet remembrancer
Now good digestion wait on appetite

And health on both

LORD
May it please your Highness sit

MACBETH
Here had we now our country's honour roofed
Were the graced person of our Banquo present
Who may I rather challenge for unkindness
Than pity for mischance

LORD
His absence Sir
Lays blame upon his promise. Please't your Highness
To grace us with your royal company

MACBETH
The table's full

LORD
Here is a place reserved Sir

MACBETH
Where

LORD
Here my good Lord
What is it that moves your Highness

MACBETH
Which of you have done this

LORD
What my good Lord

MACBETH
Thou canst not say I did it never shake
Thy gory locks at me

**LORD**
Gentlemen rise his Highness is not well

**LADY MACB**
Sit worthy friends my Lord is often thus
And hath been from his youth.  Pray you keep seat
The fit is momentary.  Are you a man

**MACBETH**
Ay and a bold one that dare look on that
Which appal the Devil

**LADY MACB**
O proper stuff
This is the very painting of your fear
This is the air-drawn dagger which you said
Led you to Duncan
Why do you make such faces. When all's done
You look but on a stool

**MACBETH**
Prithee see  there
Behold look lo how say you
Why what care I if thou canst nod speak too.
If charnel-houses and our graves must send
Those that we bury back our monuments
Shall be the jaws of kites [EXIT GHOST.]

**LADY MACB**
What quite unmanned in folly

**MACBETH**
If I stand here I saw him

**LADY MACB**
Fie for shame

**MACBETH**
The time has been

That when the brains were out the man would die
And there an end but now they rise again
With twenty mortal murthers on their crowns
And push us from our stools. This is more strange
Than such a murther is

LADY MACB
My worthy Lord
Your noble friends do lack you

MACBETH
I do forget
Do not muse at me my most worthy friends
I have a strange infirmity which is nothing
To those that know me.  Come love and health to all
Then I'll sit down give me some wine fill full [ENTER GHOST.]
I drink to the general joy of the whole table
And to our dear friend Banquo whom we miss
Would he were here to all and him we thirst
And all to all

LORDS
Our duties and the pledge

MACBETH
Avaunt and quit my sight let the earth hide thee
Thy bones are marrowless thy blood is cold
Thou hast no speculation in those eyes
Which thou dost glare with

LADY MACB
Think of this good Peers
But as a thing of custom 'tis no other
Only it spoils the pleasure of the time

MACBETH
What man dare I dare. Hence horrid shadow
Unreal mockery hence [ EXIT GHOST]
Why so being gone

I am a man again pray you sit still

LADY MACB
You have displaced the mirth
Broke the good meeting with most admired disorder

MACBETH
How can you behold such sights
And keep the natural ruby of your cheeks
When mine is blanched with fear

LORD
What sights my Lord

LADY MACB
I pray you speak not he grows worse and worse
Question enrages him at once good night
Stand not upon the order of your going
But go at once

LORD
Good night and better health
Attend his Majesty

LADY MACB
A kind good night to all [EXIT LORDS.]

MACBETH
It will have blood they say
Blood will have blood
Stones have been known to move and trees to speak
Augurs and understood relations have
By magot-pies and choughs and rooks brought forth
The secretest man of blood.  What is the night

LADY MACB
Almost at odds with morning which is which

MACBETH
How sayest thou that Macduff denies his person
At our great bidding

LADY MACB
Did you send to him Sir

MACBETH
I hear it by the way but I will send
There's not a one of them but in his house
I keep a servant fee'd. I will tomorrow
(And betimes I will ) to the Weird Sisters
More shall they speak for now I am bent to know
By the worst means the worst for mine own good
All causes shall give way. I am in blood
Stepp'd in so far that I should wade no more
returning were as tedious as go o'er
Strange things I have in head that will to hand
Which must be acted ere they may be scanned

LADY MACB
You lack the season of all natures sleep

MACBETH
Come we'll to sleep my strange and self-abuse
Is the initiate fear that wants hard use
We are yet but young in deed [ EXEUNT.]

1st LORD

...And had he Duncan's son under his key
(As and it please Heaven he shall not ) he should find
What it were to kill a father so should Banquo's son
But peace for from broad words and 'cause he failed
His presence at the tyrant's feast I hear
Macduff lives in disgrace.  Sir, can you tell
Where he bestows himself

2nd LORD

The son of Duncan
(From whom this tyrant holds the due of birth )
Lives in the English Court and is received
Of the most pious Edward with such grace
That the malvolence of Fortune nothing
Takes from his high respect. Thither Macduff
Is gone to pray the holy King for warlike aid and this report
Hath so exasperate Macbeth that he
Prepares for bloody war

1st LORD

Some holy Angel
Fly to the Court of England and unfold
His message ere he come that a swift blessing
May soon return to this our suffering country
Under a hand accursed

2nd LORD

I'll send my prayers with him [EXEUNT.]

## PART FOUR

[THUNDER.
WITCHES.]

[ Editing note: depending on how
this scene,[ down to where the WITCHES vanish,]
is to be done, it may require editing.
Given here as per original ]

1<sup>st</sup> WITCH
Thrice the brindled cat hath mewed

2<sup>nd</sup> WITCH
Thrice and once the hedge-pin whined

3<sup>rd</sup> WITCH
Harpier cries tis time tis time

1<sup>st</sup> WITCH
Round about the cauldron go
In the poisoned entrails throw
Toad that under cold stone
Days and nights has thirty one
Sweltered venom sleeping got
Boil thou first in the charmed pot

ALL
Double double toil and trouble
Fire burn and cauldron bubble

2<sup>nd</sup> WITCH
Fillet of a fenny snake
In the cauldron boil and bake
Eye of newt and toe of frog
Wool of bat and tongue of dog
Adder's fork and blind-worm's sting
Lizard's leg and howlet's wing

For a charm of powerful trouble
Like a hell-broth boil and bubble

ALL
Double double toil and trouble
Fire burn and cauldron bubble

3<sup>rd</sup> WITCH
Scale of dragon tooth of wolf
Witch's mummy maw and gulf
Of the ravined salt-sea shark
Root of hemlock digged in the dark
Liver of blaspheming Jew
Gall of goat and slips of yew
Silvered in the moon's eclipse
Nose of Turk and Tartar's lips
Finger of birth-strangled babe
Ditch-delivered by a drab
Make the gruel thick and slab
Add thereto a tiger's chaudron
For th' ingredients of our cauldron

ALL
Double double toil and trouble
Fire burn and cauldron bubble

2<sup>nd</sup> WITCH
Cool it with a baboon's blood
Then the charm is firm and good

[ENTER HACATE ]

HECATE
O well done I commend your pains
And every one shall share in the gains
And now about the cauldron sing
Like elves and fairies in a ring
Enchanting all that you put in

[ MUSIC AND SONG
*BLACK SPIRITS* etc.]

2<sup>nd</sup> WITCH
By the pricking of my thumbs
Something wicked this way comes
Open locks whoever knocks [ ENTER MACBETH]


MACBETH
How now you secret black and midnight hags
What is it you do

ALL
A deed without a name

MACBETH
I conjure you by that which you profess
(Howe'er you come to know it ) answer me
Though you untie the winds and let them fight
Against the churches though the yesty waves
Confound and swallow navigation up
Though bladed corn be lodged and trees blown down
Though castles topple on Their warders' heads
Though places and pyramids do slope
Their heads to their foundations though the treasure
Of Nature's garmen tumble all together
Even till destruction sicken answer me
To what I ask

1<sup>st</sup> WITCH
Speak

2<sup>nd</sup> WITCH
Demand

3<sup>rd</sup> WITCH
We'll answer

1<sup>st</sup> WITCH
Say if thou'dst rather hear it from our mouths
Or from our masters

MACBETH
Call 'em let me see 'em

1<sup>st</sup> WITCH
Pour in sow's blood that hath eaten
Her nine farrow grease that's sweaten
From the murtherer's gibbet throw
Into the flame

ALL
Come high or low
Thyself and office deftly show
[ THUNDER. 1<sup>st</sup> Apparition
an Armed Head]

MACBETH
Tell me thou unknown power

1<sup>st</sup> WITCH
He knows thy thought
Hear his speech but say thou nought

1<sup>st</sup> APPARITION
Macbeth Macbeth Macbeth
Beware Macduff
Beware the Thane of Fife dismiss me. Enough [DESCENDS.]

MACBETH
Whate'er thou art for thy good caution thanks
Thou hast harped my fear aright. But one word more

1<sup>st</sup> WITCH
He will not be commanded here's another
More potent than the first
[THUNDER. 2<sup>nd</sup> Apparition
A Bloody child.]

2<sup>nd</sup> APPARITION
Macbeth Macbeth Macbeth

MACBETH
Had I three ears I'd hear thee

2<sup>nd</sup> APPARITION
Be bloody bold and resolute
Laugh to scorn
The power of man for none of woman born
Shall harm Macbeth [ DESCENDS.]

MACBETH
Then live Macduff what need I fear of thee
But yet I'll make assurance double sure
And take a bond of Fate thou shalt not live
That I may tell pale-hearted Fear it lies
And sleep in spite of thunder
[ THUNDER. 3<sup>rd</sup> Apparition. A Child
crowned with a tree in his hand.]
What is this that rises like the issue of a King
And wears upon his baby-brow the round
And top of sovereignty

ALL
Listen but speak not

3<sup>rd</sup> APPARITION
Be lion-mettled proud and take no care
Who chafes who frets or where conspirers are
Macbeth shall never vanquished be until
Great Birnam Wood to high Dunsinane Hill
Shall come against him [DESCENDS›}

MACBETH
That will never be
Who can impress the forest bid the tree
Unfix his earth-bound root. Sweet bodements good
Rebellion's head rise never till the Wood
Of Birnam rise and our high-placed Macbeth
Shall live the lease of Nature pay his breath
To time and mortal custom.  Yet my heart

Throbs to know one thing tell me if your Art
Can tell so much shall Banquo's issue ever
Reign in this Kingdom

ALL
Seek to know no more

MACBETH
I will be satisfied. Deny me this
And an eternal curse fall on you let me know
Why sinks that cauldron and what noise is this [OBOES.]

1st WITCH
Show

2nd WITCH
Show

3rd WITCH
Show

ALL
Show his eyes and grieve his heart
Come like shadows so depart

[ A show of eight Kings, Banquo last
with a glass in his hand.]

MACBETH
Thou art too like the spirit of Banquo down
Thy crown does sear mine eye-balls. And thy hair
Thou other gold-bound brow is like the first
A third is like the former.  Filthy hags
Why do you show me this.  A fourth. Start eyes !
What will the line stretch out to the crack of Doom.
Another yet. A seventh. I'll see no more
And yet the eight appears who bears a glass
Which shows me many more and some I see
That two-fold balls and treble sceptres carry.

Horrible sight now I see tis true
For the blood-boltered Banquo smiles upon me
And points at them for his. What is it so

1st WITCH
Ay Sir all this is so. But why
Stands Macbeth thus amazedly
Come sisters cheer we up his sprites
And show the best of our delights
I'll charm the air to give a sound
While you perform your antics round
That this great King may kindly say
Our duties did his welcome pay

[MUSIC.
WITCHES DANCE and VANISH. ]

MACBETH
Where are they. Gone.
Let this pernicious hour
Stand aye accursed in the Calendar.
Come in without there [ ENTER a LORD.]

LORD
What's your Grace's will

MACBETH
Saw you the Weird Sisters

LORD
No my Lord

MACBETH
Came they not by you

LORD
No indeed my Lord

MACBETH
Infected be the air whereon they ride

And damned all those that trust them. I did hear
The galloping of a horse. Who was't came by

LORD
Tis two or three my Lord that bring you word
Macduff has fled to England

MACBETH
Fled to England

LORD
Ay my good Lord

MACBETH
Time, thou anticipated my dread exploits
The flighty purpose never is o'ertook
Unless the deed go with it.  From this moment
The very firstlings of my heart shall be
The firstlings of my hand. And even now
To crown my thoughts with acts be it thought and done
The Castle of Macduff I will surprise
Seize upon Fife give to the edge of the sword
His wife his babes and all unfortunate souls
That trace him in his line. No boasting like a fool
This deed I'll do before this purpose cool
But no more sights.  Where are these gentlemen
Come bring me where they are [EXEUNT.]


VOICES AT MACDUFF'S CASTLE
Murther !
Murther !
Murther !

MALCOLM and MACDUFF.]

MALCOLM

Let us seek out some desolate shade and there
Weep out our sad bosoms empty...

...

This tyrant whose sole name blisters our tongues
Was once thought honest you have loved him well

MACDUFF

I am not treacherous

MALCOLM

But Macbeth is
A good and virtuous nature may recoil
In an imperial charge

MACDUFF

I have lost my hopes

MALCOLM

Why in that rawness left you your wife and child
Those precious motives those strong knots of love
Without leave-taking.  I pray you
Let not my jealousies be your dishonours
But mine own safeties you might be rightly just
Whatever I shall think

MACDUFF

Bleed bleed poor Country
Great tyranny lay thou thy basis sure
For goodness dare not check thee wear thou thy wrongs
The title is afeered. Fare thee well Lord
I would not be the villain that thou thinkest
For the whole space that's in the tyrant's grasp
And the rich East to boot

MALCOLM

Be not offended
I speak not as in absolute fear of you

I think our country sinks beneath the yoke
It weeps it bleeds and each new day a gash
Is added to her wounds. I think withal
There would be hands uplifted in my right
And here from gracious England have I offer
Of goodly thousands. But for all this
When I shall tread upon the Tyrant's head
Or wear it on my sword yet my poor Country
Shall have more vices than it had before
More suffer and more sundry ways than ever
By him that shall succeed

MACDUFF
What should he be

MALCOLM
It is myself I mean in whom I know
All the particulars of vice so grafted
That when they shall be opened black Macbeth
Will seem as pure as snow and the poor State
Esteem him as a lamb being compared
With my confineless harms

MACDUFF
Not in the legions
Of horrid Hell can come a devil more damned
In evils to top Macbeth

MALCOLM
I grant him bloody
Luxurious avaricious false deceitful
Sudden malicious smacking of every sin
That has a name. But there's no bottom none
In my voluptuousness your wives your daughters
Your matrons and your maids could not fill up
The cistern of my lust and my desire
Better Macbeth than such a one to reign

MACDUFF
Boundless intemperance
In Nature is a tyranny it hath been
Th'untimely emptying of the unhappy throne
And fall of many Kings. But fear not yet
We have willing dames enough there cannot be
The vulture in you to devour so many
As will to greatness dedicate themselves
Finding it so inclined

MALCOLM
With this there grows
In my most ill-composed affection such
A stanchless avarice that were I King
I should cut off the Nobles for their lands
Desire his jewels and this other's house
And my more-having would be as a sauce
To make me hunger more that I should forge
Quarrels unjust against the good and loyal
Destroying them for wealth

MACDUFF
This avarice
Sticks deeper yet do not fear
Scotland hath foisons to fill up your will
Of your mere own. All these are portable
With other graces weighed

MALCOLM
But I have none. The King-becoming graces
I have no relish of them but abound
In the division of each several crime
Acting it many ways. Nay had I the power I should
Pour the sweet milk of concord into Hall
Uproar the universal peace confound
All unity on earth

MACDUFF
O Scotland Scotland

MALCOLM
If such a one is fit to govern speak
I am as I have spoken

MACDUFF
Fit to govern. No not to live. O Nation miserable !
Thy Royal Father
Was a most sainted King the Queen that bore thee
Oftener upon her knees than on her feet
Died every day she lived. Fare thee well
These evils thou repeatest upon thyself
Have banished me from Scotland.  O my breast
Thy hope ends here

MALCOLM
Macduff this noble passion
Child of integrity hath from my soul
Wiped the black scruples reconciled my thoughts
To thy good truth and honour.  Devilish Macbeth
By many of these trains hath sought to win me
Into his power and modest wisdom plucks me
From over-credulous haste but God above
Deal between thee and me for even now
I put myself in thy direction and
Unspeak mine own detraction.  Here abjure
The taints and blames I laid upon myself
For strangers to my nature. I am yet
Unknown to women never was foresworn
Scarcely have coveted that which was mine own
At no time broke my faith would not betray
The Devil to his fellow and delight
No less in truth than life. My first false speaking
Was this upon myself. What I am truly
Is thine and my poor Country's to command
Whither indeed before thy here approach
The English with ten thousand warlike men
Already at a point were setting forth

Now we'll together and the chance of goodness
Be like our warranted quarrel.  Why are you silent ?

MACDUFF
Such welcome and unwelcome things at once
Tis hard to reconcile [ENTER ROSS.]
See who comes here

MALCOLM
My countryman but yet I know him not

MACDUFF
My ever gentle cousin welcome hither

MALCOLM
I know him now.  Good God betimes remove
The means that makes us strangers

ROSS
Sir amen

MACDUFF
Stands Scotland where it did

ROSS
Alas poor country
Almost afraid to know itself. It cannot
Be called our mother but our grave
Where violent sorrow seems
A modern ecstasy the dead man's knell
Is scarce there asked for who and good men's lives
Expire before the flowers in their caps
Dying or ere they sicken

MACDUFF
O relation too nice and yet too true

MALCOLM
What's the newest grief

ROSS
That of an hour's age doth hiss the speaker
Each minute teems a new one

MACDUFF
How does my wife

ROSS
Why well

MACDUFF
And all my children

ROSS
Well too

MACDUFF
The Tyrant has not battered at their peace

ROSS
No they were well at peace when I did leave them

MACDUFF
Be not a niggard of your speech how goes it

ROSS
Your eye in Scotland
Would create soldiers make our women fight
To doff their dire distress

MALCOLM
Be it their comfort
We are coming thither gracious England hath
Lent us Lord Siward and ten thousand men
An older and a better soldier none
That Christiandom gives out

ROSS

Would I could answer
This comfort with the like. But I have words
That would be howled out in the desert air
Where hearing should not latch them

MACDUFF

What concerns they
The general cause or is it a fee-grief
Due to some single breast

ROSS

No mind that's honest
But in it shares some woe though the main part
Pertains to you alone

MACDUFF

If it is mine
Keep it not from me quickly let me have it

ROSS

Let not your ears despise my tongue for ever
Which shall possess them with the heavies sound
That ever yet they heard

MACDUFF

Humh I guess at it

ROSS

Your castle is surprised your wife and babes
Savagely slaughtered to relate the manner
Were on the quarry of these murthered deer
To add the death of you

MALCOLM

Merciful Heavens
What man ne'er pull your hat upon your brows
Give sorrow words the grief that does not speak
Whispers the o'er-fraught heart and bids it break

MACDUFF
My children too

ROSS
Wife children servants all that could be found

MACDUFF
And I must be from thence. My wife killed too

ROSS
I have said

MALCOLM
Be comforted
Let's make us medicines of our great revenge
To cure this deadly grief

MACDUFF
He has no children. All my pretty ones
Did you say All. O Hell-kite ! All
What all my pretty chickens and their dam
At one fell swoop

MALCOLM
Dispute it like a man

MACDUFF
I shall do so
But I must also feel it as a man
I cannot but remember such things were
That were most precious to me did Heaven look on
And would not take their part. For me Macduff
Fell slaughter on their souls. Heaven rest their souls

MALCOLM
Be this the whetstone of your sword let grief
Convert to anger blunt not the heart enrage it

MACDUFF

O I could play the woman with mine eye
And braggard with my tongue. But gentle Heavens
Cut short all intermission front to front
Bring thou this fiend of Scotland and myself
Within my sword's length set him if he scape
Heaven forgive him too

MALCOLM

This tune goes manly
Come go we to the King our power is ready
Our lack is nothing but our leave. Macbeth
Is ripe for shaking and the Powers above
Put on their instruments receive what cheer you may
The night is long that never finds the day

[ EXEUNT.]

## PART FIVE

[ LADY MACBETH with a taper.

Note: in Original she is watched by a
Doctor and a Woman and they talk of her
sleepwalking and obsessional washing of hands. ]

### LADY MACB
Out damned spot out I say
One two why then tis time to do it. Hell is murky.
Fie my Lord fie a soldier and afeared. What need we fear
Who knows it when none can call our power to accompt
Yet who would have thought the old man
To have so much blood in him

...

The Thane of Fife had a wife where is she now
What will these hands ne'er be clean
No more o' that my Lord no more o' that
You mar all with this starting

.....

Here's the smell of blood still
All the perfumes of Arabia will not sweeten this little hand
Oh oh oh

....

Wash your hands put on your nightgown look not so pale
I tell you yet again Banquo's buried
He cannot come out on his grave


...

To bed to bed there's knocking at the gate
Come come come come give me your hand
What's done cannot be undone
To bed to bed to bed

[ EXIT. ]

[ LENNOX and others are going
over to MALCOLM and MACDUFF's side]

LENNOX

The English power is near led on by Malcolm
His uncle Siward and the good Macduff.
Revenges burn in them for their dear causes
Would to the bleeding and the grim alarm
Excite the mortified man
Near Birnam wood
Shall we well meet them that way they are coming
While Macbeth great Dunsinane does strongly fortify
Some say he's mad others that lesser hate him
Do call it valiant fury but for certain
He cannot buckle his distempered cause
Within the belt of rule
Now does he feel
His secret murthers sticking on his hands
...
Well march we on
To give obedience where tis truly owed
Meet we the medicine of the sickly weal
And with him pour we in our country's purge
Each drop of us or so much as it needs
To dew the sovereign flower and drown the weeds
Make we our march towards Birnam
[ EXEUNT MARCHING.


MACBETH attended and a DOCTOR.]

MACBETH

Bring me no more reports let them fly all
Till Birnam wood remove to Dunsinane
I cannot taint with fear.  What's the boy Malcolm
Was he not born of woman. The spirits that know
All mortal consequences have pronounced me thus
Fear not Macbeth no man that's born of woman
Shall e'er have power over thee. Then fly false Thanes

And mingle with the English epicures
The mind I sway by and the heart I bear
Shall never sag with doubt nor shake with fear [ENTER SERVANT.]
The Devil take thee black thou cream-faced loon
Where got'st thou that goose look

SERVANT
There is ten thousand

MACBETH
Geese villain

SERVANT
Soldiers sir

MACBETH
Go prick thy face and over-red thy fear
Thou lily-livered boy. What soldiers patch.
Death of thy soul those linen cheeks of thine
Are councillors to fear. What soldiers whey-face

SERVANT
The English force so please you

MACBETH
Take thy face hence [ EXIT SERVANT.]
Seyton I am sick at heart
When I behold Seyton I say this push
Will cheer me ever or disseat me now
I have lived long enough my way of life
Is fallen into the sear the yellow leaf
And that which should accompany old age
As honour love obedience troops of friends
I must not look to have but in their stead
Curses not loud but deep mouth-honoured breath
Which the poor heart would fain deny and dare not
Seyton [ENTER SEYTON.]

78

SEYTON
What's your gracious pleasure

MACBETH
What news more

SEYTON
All is confirmed my Lord which was reported

MACBETH
I'll fight till from my bones my flesh be hacked
Give me my armour

SEYTON
Tis not needed yet

MACBETH
I'll put it on
Send out more horses skirr the country round
Hang those that talk of fear. Give me mine armour
How does your patient doctor

DOCTOR
Not so sick my Lord
As she is troubled with thick-coming fancies
That keep her from her rest

MACBETH
Cure her of that
Canst not minister to a mind diseased
Pluck from the memory a rooted sorrow
Raze out the written troubles of the brain
And with some sweet oblivious antidote
Cleanse the stuffed bosom of that perilous stuff
Which weighs upon the heart

DOCTOR
Therein the patient
Must administer to himself

MACBETH

Throw physic to the dogs I'll none of it
Come put mine armour on give me my staff
Seyton send out doctor the Thanes fly from me
Come sir dispatch.  If thou couldst doctor cast
The water of my land find her disease
And purge it to a sound and pristine health
I would applaud thee to the very echo
That should applaud again. Pull it off I say
What rhubarb senna or what purgative drug
Would scour these English hence hear'st thou of them


DOCTOR

Ay my good Lord your royal preparation
Makes us hear something


MACBETH

Bring it after me
I will not be afraid of death and bane
Till Birnam Forest come to Dunsinane


DOCTOR

Were I from Dunsinane away and clear
Profit again should hardly draw me near

[ EXEUNT.


DRUM and COLOURS.
MALCOLM, MACDUFF
LORDS and SOLDIERS Marching.]


MALCOLM

What wood is this before us


MACDUFF

The wood of Birnam


MALCOLM

Let every soldier hew him down a bough

And bear't before him thereby shall we shadow
The numbers of our host and make discovery
Err in report of us

MACDUFF
It shall be done

[ EXEUNT.

MACBETH, SEYTON and
SOLDIERS MARCHING.]

MACBETH
Hang out our banners on the outward walls
The cry is still they come our Castle's strength
Will laugh a siege to scorn here let them lie
Till famine and the ague eat them up
Were they not forced with those that should be ours
We might have met them dareful beard to beard
And beat them back home. What is that noise [A cry of women.]

SEYTON
It is the cry of women my good Lord

MACBETH
I have almost forgot the taste of fear
The time has been my senses would have cooled
To hear a night-shriek and my fell of hair
Would at a dismal treatise rouse and stir
As life were in it. I have supped full of horrors
Direness familiar to my slaughterous thoughts
Cannot once start me.  Wherefore was that cry

SEYTON
The Queen my Lord is dead

MACBETH
She should have died hereafter
There would have been a time for such a word
Tomorrow and tomorrow and tomorrow

Creeps in this petty pace from day to day
To the last syllable of recorded time
And all our yesterdays have lighted fools
The way to dusty death.  Out out brief candle
Life's but a walking shadow a poor player
That struts and frets his hour upon the stage
And then is heard no more. It is a tale
Told by an idiot full of sound and fury
Signifying nothing
[ENTER SOLDIER.]
Thou comest to use thy tongue thy story quickly

SOLDIER
Gracious my Lord
I should report that which I say I saw
But know not how to do it

MACBETH
Well say sir

SOLDIER
As I did my stand upon the hill
I looked towards Birnham and anon methought
The Wood began to move

MACBETH
Liar and slave

SOLDIER
Let me endure your wrath if it be not so
Within this three mile may you see it coming
I say a moving grove

MACBETH
If thou speakest false
Upon the next tree shalt thou hang alive
Till famine cling thee if thy speech be sooth
I care not if thou dost for me as much.
I pull in resolution and begin

To doubt the equivocation of the fiend
That lies like truth.  Fear not till Birnam Wood
Do come to Dunsinane and now a wood
Comes towards Dunsinane.  Arm arm and out
If this which he avouches does appear
There is nor flying hence nor tarrying here.
I 'gin to be weary of the sun
And wish the estate of the world were now undone.
Ring alarum-bell blow wind come wrack
At least we'll die with harness on our back

[ EXEUNT

DRUMS and COLOURS.
MALCOLM, MACDUFF and their ARMY with boughs.]

MALCOLM
Now near enough
Your leavy screens throw down
And show like those you are you worthy cousin
Lead our first battle. Worthy Macduff and we
Shall take upon's what else remains to do
According to our order

LORD
Fare you well
Do we but find the tyrant's power tonight
Let us be beaten if we cannot fight

MACDUFF
Make all the trumpets speak give them all breath
Those clamorous harbingers of blood and death
[ EXEUNT.
ALARUMS CONTINUE.

ENTER MACBETH.]
MACBETH
They have tied me to the stake I cannot fly

But bear-like must I fight the course. What's he
That's not born of woman.  Such a one
Am I to fear or none [ENTER ENGLISH LORD.]

LORD
What is thy name

MACBETH
Thou'lt be afraid to hear it

LORD
No though thou callest thyself a hotter name
Than any is in Hell

MACBETH
My name's Macbeth

LORD
The Devil himself could not pronounce a title
More hateful to mine ear

MACBETH
No nor more fearful

LORD
Thou liest abhorred Tyrant with my sword
I'll prove the lie thou speakest

[ FIGHT.
THE LORD is slain.]

MACBETH
Thou wast born of woman
But swords I smile at weapons laugh to scorn
Brandished by man that's of woman born. [EXIT.
ALARUMS.
ENTER MACDUFF.]

MACDUFF
That way the noise is Tyrant show thy face
If thou be'st slain and with no stroke of mine

84

My wife and children's ghosts will haunt me still
I cannot strike at wretched kerns whose arms
Are hired to bear their staves either thou Macbeth
Or else my sword with an unbattered edge
I sheathe again undeeded   [ EXIT.
                                        ALARUMS


ENTER MACBETH. ]


MACBETH
Why should I play the Roman fool and die
On mine own sword. Whiles I see lives the gashes
Do better upon them [ ENTER MACDUFF.]


MACDUFF
Turn Hell-hound run


MACBETH
Of all men else I have avoided thee
But get thee back my soul is too much charged
With blood of thine already


MACDUFF
I have no words
My voice is in my sword thou bloodiest villain
Than terms can give thee out
                                [ THEY FIGHT. ALARUM.]


MACBETH
Thou losest labour
I bear a charmed life which must not yield
To one of woman born


MACDUFF
Despair thy charm
And let the angel whom thou still hast served
Tell thee Macduff was from his mother's womb
Untimely ripped

MACBETH

Accursed be that tongue that tells me so
For it had cowed my better part of man
And be these juggling fiends no more believed
That palter with us in a double sense
That keep the word of promise in our ear
And break it to our hope.  I'll not fight with thee

MACDUFF

Then yield thee coward
And live to be the show and gaze o' th' time
We'll have thee as our rarest monsters are
Painted upon a pole and underwrit
Here may you see the tyrant

MACBETH

I will not yield
To kiss the ground before young Malcolm's feet
And to be baited with the rabble's curse
Though Birnam Wood be come to Dunsinane
And thou opposed being of no woman born
Yet I will try the last.  Before my body
I throw my warlike shield lay on Macduff
And damned be him that first cries hold enough

[EXEUNT FIGHTING. Alarums.
RETREAT and FLOURISH.
ENTER WITH  DRUMS and COLOURS
MALCOLM , LORDS and SOLDIERS. ]

MALCOLM

Macduff is missing and my noble cousin

[ENTER MACDUFF
with MACBETH'S HEAD.]

MACDUFF

Hail King Malcolm so thou art
Behold where stands
The usurper's cursed head the time is free
I see thee compassed with thy Kingdom's pearl

That speak their salutations in their minds
Whose voices I desire aloud with mine
Hail King of Scotland

ALL
Hail King of Scotland   [ FLOURISH.]

MALCOLM
We shall not spend a large expense of time
Before we reckon with your several loves
And make us even with you.   What's more to do
As calling home our exiled friends abroad
That fled the snares of watchful tyranny
Producing forth the cruel ministers
Of this dead butcher and his fiend-like Queen
Who (as tis thought) by self and violent hands
Took off her life. This and what needful else
That calls upon us by the grace of Grace
We will perform in measure time and place
So thanks to all at once and to each one
Whom we invite to see us crowned at Scone

[ FLOURISH.
EXEUNT OMNES. ]

## END OF THE PLAY

Printed in January 2023
by Rotomail Italia S.p.A., Vignate (MI) - Italy